# <u>Bound By Twisted Passion</u>
## By T. Brian Loos

# Bound by Twisted Passion

T. Brian Loos

Published by TBL Publishing, 2023.

BOUND BY TWISTED PASSION

**First edition. September 4, 2023.**

Copyright © 2023 T. Brian Loos.

ISBN: 979-8223731719

Written by T. Brian Loos.

# Also by T. Brian Loos

Say My Name Boy
Sir Ryan and Mark
The Miracle Drug - Crystal Meth / English & German Edition
Island of Men
My Straight Buddy
Post-WWII in Germany
The Prison Dungeon
Breeding Camp Of No Return
The Witch Broom Flight & Landing Manual for Advanced
German & English Edition
Dickipedia
Puppers Lane
Bound by Twisted Passion

People say the real love of your life happens only once in a Lifetime.

If I believe those words, then I met the love of my life already and I don't have to search for it anymore.

It began in June 2010, when I was browsing through profiles on a gay online hookup site. The picture of one profile caught my attention and I sent him a message. He messaged me back instantly and we exchanged a few small messages. We didn't have much to say and we didn't click that day. About two months later on a Sunday in August, I saw him online again. My mother had just passed away 8 days before. I had a few drinks and was looking for some distraction. He told me he was born and raised just a few blocks away from where I was living.

At that time he was in a homeless shelter about eight hundred miles north of me. He told me he wanted to come back to Florida, but didn't have a place to stay. His boyfriend had just broken up with him six months before. I asked him if he wants to stay with me for awhile. He couldn't believe his luck, that a stranger he just met online invited him to stay in his house.

"Ok, give me a few, I check out when and how I can come down there. My name is Rob by the way".

We exchanged phone numbers and I figured I would never hear from him again. But a half hour later he called me to let me know that he bought a Greyhound bus ticket and will arrive in three days, Wednesday night.

MY EXCITEMENT GREW with every day and when Wednesday finally was there, I was nervous. In a few hours I would meet this handsome, sexy man with his manly voice.

Around five pm I left the house. It would take me about one hour to get to the Greyhound bus station. When I got there, I parked my truck in front of the entrance. It didn't take thirty seconds for him to come outside. He was wearing a baseball cap, jeans and a plaid country shirt. He was six feet tall, 170 pounds, hairy chest and had a nicely trimmed beard.I jumped out of the truck and walked towards him.

"Hey, you must be Rob, I'm Brian". We put his suitcase in the back of the truck, jumped in the cabin and drove towards home.

"Hey, can we stop at a Liquor store, I got about forty bucks. We could get some booze and get drunk and have some fun tonight" Rob asked me. I liked the idea, so we stopped at a Liquor store close to home and got cigarettes and beer.

When we finally pulled into the garage we grabbed everything in the truck and put the beer in the fridge. I showed him the house and the bedroom where he left his suitcase and took his cloth off. I got naked simultaneously, I like to be nude whenever I can. We were chilling on the living room couch, smoked and had a lot of beers. Maybe one hour went by when Rob went down on the floor and kneeled between my legs.

"I'm sorry Rob but I usually can't get hard when I drink alcohol", I explained to him, but he didn't mind.

"Same here, it goes up and down, but I like to suck on a soft cock".

He took my dick in his mouth and sucked it for quite awhile, but I couldn't get a hard on. It felt great anyway. "Hey you want to try the electro stim box on me now, you told me on the phone you would" Rob asked me.

"Sure, whatever you want to try, I have a few toys in my nightstand. I went into the bedroom and took all my toys out of the drawer. I went back into the living room and showed them to Rob. First we tried electro stim on him. I pushed a metal sound down his urethra and connected the wire to the box. As a second electrode we choose a metal butt plug. I pushed it into Rob's ass and connected it also to the estim box. I turned the power on and slowly turned it up.

"Just turn it up higher, you can't hurt me" I heard Rob saying. So I did. He started moaning and I saw precum oozing out of the tip of his cock head, even with the metal rod stuffed inside his cock. After awhile my ass hole started twitching and I wanted to feel his cock inside of me. He turned on his back and I was riding his dick until he asked me if I want him to cum inside of me. Of course I wanted him to fill me up with his hot semen. I could feel his cock starting to pulse and spurt a load into my fuck hole. I stroked my uncut cock as fast as I could and shot my cum all over his hairy chest and belly.

THE BEER MADE US BOTH tired and very soon he fell asleep on the couch and the same happened to me.

I cuddled up to him and my dick was touching his ass crack. That's all I remember from that night.

Next morning around five AM he woke up and grabbed another beer out of the fridge. I had my first beer about five hours later and pretty soon we had to get more beer from the corner store. The day went by drinking passer, being naked and watching porn. Later in the day I made dinner when Rob came into the kitchen, stroking his cock and asked me:

"HEY YOU WANT TO WATCH me jerking off and shoot my load on the counter" ?

"Hell yea, some creamy protein on the mashed potatoes gives a good taste", I answered. Rob stepped right next to me and kept stroking his dick. I got so turned on, I had to join him.

I pulled my foreskin back, grabbed a piece of butter from the counter and lubed up my cock.

We both kept stroking until Rob was moaning and breathing louder. He sprayed his seed all over the black granite countertop followed by me ten seconds later. I shot my cum right next to his cum puddle. I used my middle finger and mixed our cum together. Rob was still squeezing the last drops out of his dick, when he suddenly bent down and licked our cum of the countertop.

He still had his mouth full of sperm, grabbed my head and gave me a kiss. I opened my mouth and Rob fed me our cum into my mouth. I swallowed every little bit of it.

"Damn that was hot, I'm feeling better now", Rob said and smiled at me.

I finished dinner and we ate outside on the porch. Rob was feeding me some mashed potatoes with his fork, but before he reached my mouth, it fell of the fork and landed on my dick.

"Want me to lick it clean for you," Rob asked me. Before I could answer him, his head was already down on my lap, his tongue swirled around my dick head and cleaned it like a pro.

After a few more days of drinking, we would finally sober up.

I had my own lawn service business and Rob agreed to help with work instead of contributing money for living expenses. The next five days we worked together cutting grass or doing other yard work. We had the spontaneous idea going to Fort Lauderdale the following weekend.

We left Saturday morning at six AM and arrived around 11 AM at a friends house, where we rented a room for two nights. Early afternoon we wanted to check out a raunchy gay leather bar before we went out at night to cruise a few more bars. There are plenty to choose from in the gay district of Fort Lauderdale.

The bar was dim lit, floor and walls were painted black. There was one bar inside and another bar outside for the raunchier kind of guests.

Across from the inside bar was a cage and a dark play area. Rob and I ordered our first drink inside. We were sitting at the bar, when a drunk guy came over to us and introduced himself as Chris.

"You're a hot guy, I want to eat your ass for hours. You like having your ass rimmed", Chris asked me.

"Sure, why not. We can go to the restroom or doing it in front of everybody outside. I'm sure the guys would love to watch. For twenty bucks my ass is yours for ten minutes", I answered Chris.

"Fuck yeah, let's go outside, have another drink and I go to work on your hot ass" Chris said and he pulled a twenty dollar bill out of his pocket and gave it to me.

I was just joking about the twenty bucks but since he had no problem paying me, I took the money.

Chris and I walked outside and ordered another drink at the outside bar. Rob stayed inside and talked to a short guy standing next to him. When I was almost done with my drink, I pulled my pants down, bent over and Chris started to rim my fuck hole like a pro.

The guys standing around the bar came closer to see every detail. Chris made my hole wet and slippery and without any warning, he pushed his tongue into my ass.

It felt fucking great and I got paid for it. A few guys watched us with growing excitement. Three of them took their cocks out and started stroking. Chris noticed them and pulled down his pants.

He played with his hard cock, when one of the guys stepped behind him, spit on Chris ass hole and pushed his fat cock inside it. Chris let out a short muffled cry which became soon a soft moaning. Every time the guy slammed his dick deep inside Chris's ass, I could feel the plow extending through his tongue and pushing it deeper in my fuck tube.

Another man standing right next to me grabbed my penis and pulled my foreskin back and fore, faster and faster.

His cock was rock hard and it was obvious, he needed to release his cum. He pushed his dick into my mouth and I began to suck on it like crazy. I heard the man fucking Chris moaning louder and he sprayed his seed inside Chris's ass.

I stopped sucking on the guys dick, when he pulled out of my mouth and positioned his fuck pole behind Chris's hole and pushed it in. He did only two plows and he couldn't hold his cum any longer. He shot his load inside Chris and mixed his cum with the other guy's semen. I noticed he didn't pull out after unloading. I heard Chris mumbling :"Oh my god, he's pissing in my ass. I think I'm going to burst". At this point he stopped rimming my ass. I turned around and watched him getting filled up with fresh hot beer piss. When the guy finished emptying his bladder into Chris's ass he pulled out and asked the bartender for a funnel. He told me to lay down on my stomach. He inserted the funnel with the small end into my ready hole.

Chris was told to squat with his ass above the funnel and push the two cum loads mixed with piss, out of his ass into the funnel. He must've pushed real hard because I heard a loud splash and the content of his bowels was gushing into the funnel. The cum and piss mix was running down the funnel into my rectum.

I had to go to the men's room to clean myself up. When I was done cleaning my fuck chute I went back inside to see what Rob was doing.

He was still talking to some people and exchanging phone numbers.

"Hey Rob, you should have come outside too, you missed a hot show", I told Rob.

"Damn, why didn't you call me", he asked. "Let's go back to the room and chill for a few before we go out tonight". I agreed. We left the bar and jumped into my truck. When we got close to the house where we rented our room, Rob said : "I like you and I have some kind of feelings for you".

I told him, I could fall for him very easy myself.

We arrived at the house and went in our room.

"Hey we still have a gallon of wine in the fridge", Rob reminded me.

We finished the wine in only three hours and we both fell asleep.

When I woke up around five am next morning, I was laying in my own vomit.

"Morning Brian, did you sleep well, I had to wipe your vomit off the carpet last night but obviously you barfed again", Rob was telling me.

We had no chance to see a few more bars last night because we got too drunk in our room.

We decided to drive back home that day and save the few bucks we had left. But before I wanted to talk to Rob again about the feelings I had for him. While we were packing our few things I told him, that I'm already falling for him.

Rob looked at me and said: "I like you a lot but I don't want to get into a relationship so soon again.

I got hurt many times and it is only six month ago since my ex and I broke up. Sometimes it is better to be just friends."

I can't handle rejection very well and I was angry that I told him about my feelings.

On the way home we both didn't talk much. There was some kind of awkwardness in the air. He felt bad and guilty because he hurt my feelings and I felt sad because he didn't have the same feelings for me as I had for him. When we got back home, life was back to normal. Rob asked me the same night: "Are we good ? Can we be just friends"?

I said yes, I figured better be friends than losing him. The bad thing was, I got jealous every time he hooked up with somebody online or in a bar.

The next three month went by with no major events. We went to the local gay bar two or three times a month, drank at home and he did his hook ups once a while. Mostly when he was drinking.

I had booked a flight for us both in November to Germany. I had to go and visit family and my mother's grave, since I was unable to go to her funeral in August. I asked Rob if he wants to come with me and of course he said yes. We could stay at a friends house and one of my aunts gave us her car to drive around.

The longer Rob and I lived together, the more we found out about things we had in common.

We both loved Mercedes-Benz and we decided we going to rent one for one day when we get to Germany.

Finally the day of our departure was there. After a ten hour flight we arrived in Frankfurt Germany around eleven o'clock in the morning. We stepped outside the airport to have a cigarette while waiting for my friend to pick us up.

"Hey look Brian, the Mercedes in his natural habitat. We are finally in Benz land," Rob said to me. He saw all the taxis in front of the airport, which are usually Mercedes in Germany.

We waited about ten minutes until my friend arrived. I didn't see him since I left Germany twelve years ago. We got into his small car and left the airport. It was about a thirty minute drive to my friends place.

When we were on the Autobahn Rob asked me: "Brian is this the Autobahn ? Look the city of Ausfahrt must be very big. Since fifteen minutes I see signs with Ausfahrt."

I started laughing and explained to him: "Ausfahrt means exit, dumbass." We all were laughing about his cute comment.

When we arrived at my friends house, all three of us got naked and had a few welcome beers.

I was sitting between Rob and my friend Jochen on the couch. After a few beers, Jochen put some porn on. I thought it won't be much longer and he wants to fuck around. I was right. He put his hand between my legs and pulled my foreskin back and played with my cock head. Rob got up and kneeled in front of Jochen and sucked his cock while pulling Jochens foreskin back and fore with his lips. We all threw a boner and precum was oozing out of our cocks.

"Hey Rob," I said," I want to dock your cock."

I didn't have to tell him twice and he got off his knees and stood in front of me, pressing the tip of his dick head against mine. Our heads were slippery from the precum and I pulled my foreskin over his head. It was hot, feeling his head under my foreskin. I began to stroke our cocks with my right hand. Jochen watched for a moment but got too excited to just watch. He stepped behind Rob and with one powerful thrust he pushed his cock in his ass. Rob was moaning like hell. I stroked his and my cock faster. I could feel his dick pulsing in my hand and when he finally bucked his hips, he shot his load under my foreskin. It was so hot to watch, that it didn't take me much longer and I also sprayed my seed, mixing it with his cum underneath my foreskin. When I pulled my skin back our two loads splashed on the laminate floor and made a big puddle of cum. The smell of cum and male muskiness in the room was intoxicating.

Jochen was still pounding Robs fuck tube like crazy. But when he saw Rob and me cuming, he couldn't hold back any longer and released his hot load inside of Rob.

It must have been a big load because when Jochen pulled out, I saw some cum drops falling on the floor.

"Hold it in Rob," I said.

"I'm sure Jochen wants to enjoy his own cum in a way he probably never did before."

I told Jochen to lay down on his back.

"Rob you remember what we talked about a few weeks ago"?

"I sure do," Rob answered.

Rob squatted over Jochen, his ass hole lined up with his nose. Then he pushed the cum load out of his ass.

With my right index finger I scooped up some cum and pushed it up Jochens nostrils. He automatically snorted it up his nose and when it was running down his throat, he had to swallow it.

"Well that was some hot shit," Jochen said, still out of breath.

All three of us went into the bathroom and took a shower together. I soaped up Jochens back and butt crack. I couldn't help myself, but I got hard again. Of course Jochens uncut cock got stiff too. I thought, since I already soaped up his ass I should fuck him right there in the shower. And I did. I spread his ass cheeks and put my dick head on his hole and pushed it in. He was tight and for a few seconds he was in pain. He tried to escape my cock but I was holding him by his hips and pulled him back, pushing my penis in balls deep. Now the pain subsided and changed into pleasure.

"Get behind me Rob, we do a chain fuck. I want you to fuck me silly," I said to Rob.

He scooted behind me and fingered my hole to get it ready for his penis. "Just ram it in," I told him. And he did. I had to hold my breath so I wouldn't scream because of pain or pleasure,

I can't remember what it was. All three of us pushed our hips back and fore and fucked each other faster and faster. I injected my semen first into Jochen and when Rob felt my fuck tube tighten up, he filled me up with his sperm.

"Damn, we should be empty now", Rob said.

I turned around and looked in Rob's eyes. "Yes and you know, we should keep it inside of us and let the body absorb each others cum overnight. Well at least that's what I do."

The next morning Jochen had to go to work. He was a truck driver, sometimes he came home the same night and sometimes he was on the road for two or three days.

Rob wanted to see a castle and a palace. I showed him an old medieval castle built in 1350 only 15 minutes away from our place. It was cold that day, only 24 F and the castle was not heated. Rob and I climbed up a narrow staircase but he turned around before we got upstairs. Instead of upstairs we went downstairs and checked out the torture chamber.

I was laying down on a rack, where both legs and arms were tied to a steel bar. On the side of the rack was a crank to move both bars apart and stretch a body until the joints popped out there sockets.

"I want to fuck on that thing or at least getting sucked off," I said to Rob.

"How can you even think about sex in this creepy environment," he answered back.

But it was too cold anyway to pull my pants down.

"I need to go back to the car and turn the heat on, Rob."

"Ok, I'm coming, it's really too cold to be outside."

The two weeks went by in a breeze. Two days before we had to go back home to Florida, we visited the Christmas market in Frankfurt. It was so crowded there, we hardly could walk without bumping into other people.

Jochen took one day off work and gave us a ride to the airport on our last day. We hugged each other and promised to visit soon again. Then we had to go through security and towards the gate where our plane departed.

Back home, I had to do work for a few customers the next day. Rob said, he was too tired to get up and help.

"That's ok, I can do it myself, it won't take long," I responded to his half asleep mumbling. He slept on the couch that night. He used to sleep with me in my bed, but since I told him my feelings I had for him, he slept more often on the couch. When I asked him why he just said, because we are no boyfriends and shouldn't sleep in the same bed.

"Than we shouldn't have sex together either," I said and regretted it immediately what I just had said.

But I never give up hope. I thought maybe one day, when he is over his ex, we both could be together as boyfriends.

I loved him so much.

I hurried up to get to my customers so I would be back before it gets too hot in the afternoon. I got back home around two, took a shower in the garage bathroom and walked naked into the kitchen and living room.

Rob was sitting on the couch and a guy was lying on Rob's legs. Both were also naked and Rob was stroking that guys cock. They didn't hear me coming in so I was hiding in the kitchen where they couldn't see me but I could watch them. Rob put more lube on that guy's cock and stroked it really fast. The guy was not hairy at all but had a few nice tattoos on his legs, chest and arms. He was breathing faster and screamed: "I'm going to shoot my fucking jizz dude," and his sperm splashed on his stomach. How could I not play with my cock and jerk off, watching Rob and whoever that guy was. I sprayed my cum on the kitchen floor two seconds after the guy shot his load. I think I was breathing to loud or my foreskin made some stroking noises but somehow they heard me cumming. Rob got off the couch and walked into the kitchen. I had to escape back into the garage. I didn't want them to know I watched. When Rob got into the kitchen, he saw my cum puddle on the floor and knew, it had to be my cum. He scooped it up with his finger and went back to the dude on the couch. He put his finger under the guy's nose and had him sniff my cum. Then the guy licked my seed of Rob's finger. It was so hot I almost wanted to jerk off again.

But now the feeling of jealousy crawled up my spine. Why had Rob sex with this guy instead of having fun with me ? What did this guy have that I didn't ? I put my shorts on and walked into the living room. The dude felt uncomfortable, it was clearly noticeable, and I enjoyed it.

I couldn't help myself and yelled at Rob :"What's he doing here ? Get him out of here. In ten minutes he's gone."

I went into the bedroom and lay down on the bed. After the guy left, Rob came into the bedroom and sat on the floor next to the bed.

"I'm sorry Brian, don't be mad. But I'm a single gay man and you shouldn't get mad and jealous when I have somebody over. I'm really sorry that I can't give you what you want. I love you but not in a romantic way."

I saw some tears in his eyes and I knew he really meant it. During the next few month I was drinking more often and it started to affect my business. I lost a few customers but it wasn't enough to be worried. Robs mood started to change in between minutes more often. I knew he had issues with depression and bipolarism in the past but it was never that obvious.

I decided to look for a roommate and rent out the spare bedroom. This way we had extra money coming in. The business didn't bring in as much money as it used to. It didn't take long, maybe about five days, and somebody answered the ad about the room for rent. He called and asked if he could stop by after work to look at the room. He had a sexy manly voice and I was curious what he would look like.

At five pm he was at the front door. I opened the door and there was this thirty-nine-year-old man with a goatee, a tattoo on his right forearm, and a baseball cap.

"Hi, I'm Jim. I called earlier about the room," he said. I thought, wow he is a sexy little fucker. We went outside and were sitting on the porch. He talked about him, his work, and that he and his boyfriend just broke up one day ago. We even forgot to look at the room until he was ready to leave to get his stuff from his ex's apartment. When he came back one hour later, we put his clothes and computer into his room. He needed to go to the store to get food. I had to go too, so we both went together. I liked him and we both clicked. The next morning he went to work but when he came back at five pm he told me, he and his ex were talking during his lunch break and he was driving back in with him. He already paid for two weeks rent but he wanted me to keep it in case he has to come back if they would argue again. And they argued again and he came back.

That night Rob had a trick over again. I was with Jim in his room talking about his and my life. Rob was in the master bedroom with his guest. Jim asked me about Rob, if we both are together. So I told him the story about Rob and me. He asked me if I wanted to stay with him in his room overnight since Rob was in my bedroom doing his hook up. Of course I wanted and we both got naked and snuggled up in his bed. There is no snuggling without getting a boner, for me at least. I reached around him and grabbed his penis. We both got excited, it was our first time together. I could feel his hard cock poking my ass. I pushed back on his dick and with both my hands I spread my ass cheeks apart. He lubed up my hole and his dick. He pushed his pole hard into my fuck hole and all the way in. His cock felt great inside of me and he started to tear my ass apart. He was reaching around me, pulled my foreskin back and rubbed my dick head between his thumb and index finger. His dick had the right size and angle to hit my prostate, he fucked the precum right out of me. I rolled over on my stomach and Jim got on top of me. He put his right arm around my neck and was holding me tight while he pumped his cock deep into my hole. He shot three big spurts followed by me, spraying my cum on his bed sheets.

The next morning we got up together and made coffee. We were cuddling on the couch while having a cigarette with our coffee.

I dropped Jim off at work, I had to go to the store and to work myself anyway. When Jim came home from his job around five pm, he told me and Rob, he is going back to his ex again to give it another try.

From that day on, Jim came over to my house every day on his lunch break. We fucked for one hour and then he went back to work with a smile on his face.

One day after lunch break he didn't feel like going back to work. He wanted to stay with me in bed all afternoon and cuddle.

"Do you think you could fall for me ? I think I'm already falling for you," Jim said to me.

"Yes I feel the same way," I responded.

To say I love him would have been too soon, but I definitely had feelings for him. But how could I commit to someone when I still had Rob on my mind. I loved all my exes, but with Rob it was different, more intense.

I thought a relationship with someone would maybe help me to get over Rob.

At five pm he had to go home so his partner would think he came home from work. He told me he would leave him soon and move in with me. I asked him why he is not leaving him now , when this is his plan anyway. He told me after Thanksgiving, which was only one week away.

He invited Rob and me to come to there house on Thanksgiving day and have dinner.

Rob and I arrived around four pm on Thanksgiving at Jim's place. We were sitting outside until the turkey was done. Jim had the idea to go with me to the liquor store to get some booze. We got in his truck and drove to the nearby store and parked in front of it.

"Give me a kiss before we go inside," Jim said to me. I gave him a long kiss and pushed my tongue into his mouth. He was chewing gum and when we were done kissing, I had his gum in my mouth.

"That's what I call a kiss you pig," I mumbled and smiled at him. We bought a bottle of blackberry liqueur and went back to his place. Rob was still sitting outside with Nick, Jimmy's partner. Jim and I took advantage of the situation and acted like we would cook together. We were standing in one kitchen corner and kissed again. From there Jimmy took me into their spare bedroom while Rob still distracted Nick. Jimmy dropped his pants and was laying down on the floor. He was already hard as a rock. He didn't have to tell me what to do. I opened my zipper and my pants came down. I lowered my ass, lined up his cock on my fuck hole and took a seat on it. I couldn't get hard, even I was shaking for excitement. The thought his boyfriend could come in made me nervous. I was riding up and down on his cock and Jimmy stroked my dick with his right hand. I was almost about to lose my load, when I heard somebody coming in from outside and towards the bathroom which was right next to the room we were in. Jimmy lost his boner and I lost my load. My cum sprayed all over Jimmy's stomach. I tried not to moan or make any noises but I heard a deep roaring sound coming from my throat. I had never before heard something like it. The steps stopped in the hallway and then came closer to the bedroom door. I jumped off Jimmy's cock as fast as I could and tried to pull up my pants.

"What are you fuckers doing here, are you both out of your mind," I heard Rob saying. "Nick is about to go to the bathroom. I thought I go before him and check what's going on. You both disappeared quite a while ago. And I'm tired to entertain him by myself."

"Ok we're coming. Actually I already did cum," I whispered with a grin.

"Don't be a smart ass and get out of here," Rob mumbled and went into the bathroom.

Jim and I sneaked back into the kitchen and continued cooking. Fifteen minutes later the turkey and side dishes were ready. We all sat down at the dinner table and Jimmy cut a few slices of the turkey. Everybody ate like there is no tomorrow.

"It was very delicious, thank you Jim. I'm stuffed and tired now," Rob said.

"Yeah I think everybody is getting sleepy, let's go home before we overstay our welcome," I added and blinked my left eye, looking at Jimmy.

He gave me and Rob enough food for the next five days to take home.

When we got back to my house Rob wanted to talk to me.

"Don't you think he's going to cheat on you the same way he is cheating on his ex, partner or whatever he is ? Think about it before you get too involved. You can do a lot better than him," Rob said to me. I knew Jimmy was a slut but I thought I could handle it.

The following week Rob was doing some handyman work for an older lady. We could use the extra income. I couldn't pay my mortgage since ten month and the bank threatened with foreclosure. On the third day he worked for her, he came home with four hundred dollars. I thought damn, she is a generous lady. Around six pm the doorbell rang and there was the older lady standing outside.

"Don't open the door, she maybe gave me more money than she wanted and now she noticed it and wants some of it back," Rob was whispering. It was too late, I already had turned the doorknob and opened the door. Rob disappeared somewhere.

"Hi I'm Miss Snyder. Rob was working for me. Are you his roommate," she asked me.

"Yes I am, how can I help you ?"

She told me her credit card disappeared and the bank informed her that four hundred dollars were withdrawn at an ATM machine two hours ago. She also said, she thinks Rob took her card and already called the police. I told her Rob isn't home at the moment but I will certainly let him know. After she left, Rob came back inside from the garage and had tears in his eyes. He heard everything she said. He was afraid he had to go to jail and that I would throw him out of my house. But I couldn't help myself when I saw him crying. I hugged him and told him, it doesn't matter to me what he did. He was somewhat relieved and thanked me with a kiss on my lips. My dick got semi hard the same second. That was the first time he kissed me after I told him in Fort Lauderdale about the feelings I had for him.

We decided, to put my house on the market. It would be better to sell and get some money out of it than have the bank foreclose on it. The real estate agent came over and looked at the house a few days later. I gave the ok to list it for eighty thousand dollars. Robs mother gave him and me a house free and clear with no mortgage to pay.

Rob and I started packing everything we didn't need on a daily basis. It must have been about two weeks later, when two cops were at the front door asking for Rob. They asked him a few questions about the credit card incident and before I knew, Rob was in handcuffs and on the back seat of the cruiser.

They brought him to the closest jail about sixteen miles away. Unfortunately I didn't have the money to bail him out. I was crying when I was thinking about Rob being in jail. The court date was set for twenty five days later. In the meantime the realtor found a buyer for my house. Jimmy was helping me moving the last stuff and a few furniture to the new house. He moved in with me after him and Nick had an argument again.

I visited Rob every Friday in jail and he was always happy to see me. He told me about his daily routine in jail and I told him about the progress I made with the sale of the house and other things.

On the first weekend after we officially moved into the new house, Jimmy and I spent Saturday and Sunday at a gay campground not far from us.

We rented a small cabin with two queen size beds and a refrigerator close to the heated pool. The entire campground was clothing optional. For Saturday night they had a play area or so called 'deviants fetish den' set up. We spent all day at the pool, had a few drinks and enjoyed the sight of naked men in the sun. The night couldn't come soon enough. We wanted to go to the play area at midnight and get really piggy.

I thought about Rob again, wondering how he was doing. I had a bit of a bad conscience enjoying myself, knowing that Rob was in jail. But he probably would be out soon. The court date was in nine days.

Finally it was midnight and Jimmy and I walked over to the den. At the entrance they served free beer to get the guys primed up. We walked inside and there was a chair on a pedestal, a bathtub, a wooden cross, a cage, several slings and a separate small room with glory holes in the wall. On the floor was hay spread out for whatever reason. Most guys were naked and some wore only shorts with their dicks and balls hanging out. I walked around and watched a hairy bear getting flogged at the cross. I looked at his cock to see how excited he was. His dick was fat and veiny, dripping precum in a steady flow with every hit he got with the whip. I bent down and took his cock head into my mouth. His precum tasted sweet and salty and I made sure I cleaned the head very well. While I bent down my fuck hole was visible to everybody. A tall guy behind me stuck his middle finger into my ass hole and massaged my prostate. I could feel my precum oozing out of my dick and dripping down on the floor. I was getting hard and had to stroke my cock. Jimmy came over and watched us for a while. Then he said to the guy handling the whip :

"Hit his fucking cock head with the whip and make him whimper. I want to know if it makes him harder or soft."

I stopped sucking the precum from the bears dick and the guy with the whip went to work. He hit the poor bears cock head hard with the first hit. The hairy bear screamed loud when the whip plowed down on his head. With the second and third hit his cock got actually harder and he started to pump out a big load of jizz which splashed in all directions with each hit of the whip. By then seven men were standing around watching and stroking their cocks. The bear was done and I went over to the sling area. To get there I had to pass the bathtub where one guy was sitting inside of it and five other guys standing around and pissed on him. He tried to get as much piss in his mouth as possible. The sling action seemed more interesting to me. One guy was lying in a sling and got fucked hard. The other guy got fisted by a tall muscled man with tattoos on his arms and legs. He had his right arm almost to the elbow inside the guy's rectum. It seemed like they both were really into it. The man who got fisted was moaning and his cock was hard as a rock. Every time the tattooed guy moved his hand inside of his ass, his dick jerked and drippings of precum were oozing out of his piss slit. I wanted to feel that cock inside of me. I climbed on top of him, grabbed his cock and when I felt his fat purple head on my hole, I lowered myself down until the eighth inches disappeared in my ass. His precum was the perfect lube. I was riding his cock hard and the muscled guy gave him a good prostate massage from the inside. The poor guy couldn't hold back his cum any longer and seeded my fuck tube with his massive hot load. I stroked my cock as fast as I could, pulled my foreskin back and fore until I exploded on his stomach. The tattooed guy pulled his arm out of his ass and slammed his dick inside followed by his fist again. It took him only a few plows and he jizzed deep inside. I still had his cock inside of me and could feel another load filling me up even more. I raised my ass up until his fat dick slapped down on his belly. Two cum loads leaked out of my freshly fucked hole and dripped on his nut sack, running down to his ass and coated the tattooed guys cock. "Thanks' guys, that was fucking hot," I said to them both. I needed a break and walked back to the entrance to get myself a beer.

THERE WAS JIMMY KNEELING on the ground and stroked his cock with his right hand. One man had a funnel and inserted it in Jimmy's hungry hole. He took a pitcher of beer and filled it in the funnel, from where it was running down into Jim's already cum filled hole. Seven horny men were standing around him, watching and jerking their meat to the hot scene. When Jimmy couldn't take any more liquid up his ass, he got up on his legs and walked over to the bath tub. He was in a hurry, he couldn't hold it all in for much longer. He turned his ass hole towards the slave sitting in the tub and let loose. Beer and semen mixed together were gushing out of Jimmy's pucker and covered the pig slave in a smelly mess. The smell of sperm, beer, ass and man sweat in the room was intoxicating.

The men standing around the tub jerked off and covered the slave in seventeen jizz loads. Then a few of them started to lick the beer-cum mixture off the pig slave until he was clean.

It was already four am and they had to close the fetish den. Jimmy and I walked back to our cabin.

"Brian look what I found, somebody's briefs. And we get to sniff on it," Jimmy said to me. The front part that covers the dick and nuts had one crusty cum stain on it.

I sniffed the cum stain, put it in my mouth until it was soaking wet and sucked the cum out of it.

"You are such a nasty slut. But that's one part of you I love," Jimmy said.

The next day we had to go back home. It was a fun weekend I got to spent with Jimmy. He mentioned he would like to get our own place before Rob comes back home from jail.

The next few days I had some customers lined up. Friday was the last day I could visit Rob in jail before his court date.

From two to three pm was visitation time. I told Rob about me and Jimmy trying to find our own place and everything else that happened during the past week.

Rob was kind of quiet that day. We had only ten minutes visitation left, when Rob said :

"I don't want you to move out with Jim."

I didn't know what to say, I was speechless. All I came up with was "Why"? and Rob continued talking.

"I love you, I don't want you to go and move in with this Jim. I had a lot of time to think about us, relationships and all that. I want you and me to be together. When I get out of here, we stay three days in our bedroom. Make sure we have enough lube."

Now I was really stunned and surprised. I had tears in my eyes and Rob saw it.

"You make me the happiest man on earth Rob but let's talk more about it when you get home. I got to go, it's already three o'clock."

"Ok Brian, only a few more days. I hope so. If they put me on probation. If not I have to stay in here for at least five more month."

"Don't even think about it Rob. Of course you get on probation. Ok, got to go. See you in court."

On my way home, my mind was running on high speed. What happened in jail that made Rob change his attitude towards relationships and me. What I going to do. The man I love more than anything just told me he loves me and wants to be with me. But there was also Jimmy.

When I got home, Jimmy wasn't there. I found a note on my desk : 'Hey Brian, I have to stay with Nick for awhile. He needs my help right now. Will stay in touch. Love always, Jimmy.'

Normally I would be angry and sad after reading his note, but I wasn't, and I felt bad about it. Rob was probably right when he told me Jimmy is a slut and will never change. He also said I could do much better.

But I always say, everything happens for a reason.

I couldn't wait for Rob's court date. Monday morning at 8.30 I left the house. Court started at nine. I found a seat in one of the front rows. The deputies brought the inmates into the courtroom. There was Rob. For the first time I saw him in handcuffs. Somehow it turned me on and I felt my cock and ass hole twitching. But nothing I could do about it. After 40 minutes Rob's case was called. Rob and his public defender stepped in front of the judge and waited for the sentence. One year probation and payment of $ 400.- restitution was the judge's order.

Rob and I were happy. We could be home together that night. Between midnight and two am is usually the time when the jail releases people. At 1.30 am Rob called me.

"Hey babe, I'm free. You can come and pick me up and don't forget to bring cigarettes please."

"I'm on my way, give me thirty minutes."

I was ready to leave in five minutes and arrived at the jail 25 minutes later. Rob was already waiting for me in the parking lot. He jumped into the truck and was lighting a cigarette. It was kind of an awkward situation. It was the first time we were together as boyfriends and neither Rob or I were sure how to react in that situation. I thought when we get home we will break the ice in our bedroom.

We arrived at home and Rob looked around the house. It was the first time he saw all furniture's set up and the house decorated.

"Good job, it looks really nice babe," Rob said and looked into my eyes. He gave me a long and passionate kiss. "Well it's about time you kiss me," I mumbled and grinned at him. "I bet you are starving for some bedroom attention, don't you ?" I asked him.

"No not really, I jerked off with one guy in jail before they released me. I'm kidding babe," he was joking.

I couldn't wait any longer. When I just looked at Rob and the bulge between his legs, it gave me an instant boner.

"Come on Rob, let's have some wild crazy sex. If you want we can have a threesome and we both get fucked or whatever happens. And tomorrow we make love, just you and me. How does that sound ?"

"Sounds tempting to me you horny little fucker. Let's go online and see what we can find," Rob answered.

We actually found a guy living very close to us with a big ten inch cock.

Rob and I were already naked, when we opened the door for the guy. He introduced himself as Jarold. We walked straight into the bedroom where he dropped his cloth and his big fat cock was swinging in front of his huge nuts.

"Let's go to work," was all he said and Rob was already on his hands and knees. Jarold fingered Rob's ass, opened it up and got it ready for his big fat cock. With one powerful thrust, he slammed his cock balls deep into Rob's ass. Rob screamed but I didn't know if it was for pleasure or pain. I knew it must have been for pain when I saw Rob trying to escape that huge cock. But Jarold grabbed him by his hips and pulled him back on his cock. The pain subsided and Rob started moaning and playing with his dick. Jarold kept pumping his meat into Rob's stretched fuck hole and with each hard thrust, he fucked Rob's head against the bedroom wall. I laid on my back and slid underneath Rob. I tied up Rob's nut sack with a rubber band. This way I could get a good grip on his tight balls. I put my mouth underneath his cock and his precum dripped on my tongue. When I had a good amount of precum in my mouth, I took Rob's cock head between my lips and each thrust of Jarold's cock pushed Rob's dick into my mouth.

Rob was so overstimulated, he could not hold his cum any longer.

"Yeah, babe I want your seed. Give me your hot cum," I said as good as I could with his dick in my mouth.

Rob nodded and his semen shot to the back of my throat. I swallowed some of it. I loved the taste of Rob's cum, slightly bitter sweet. He pulled his cock out of my mouth because his head became very sensitive after he lost his load. I moved close to his mouth and gave him a kiss. We both opened our mouth and he licked his sperm off my tongue. It was such a hot and love filled moment, my cock began to jerk and released a big cum fountain through my piss slit. Jarold was still humping Rob's fuck tube but Rob couldn't take his big cock any more after he ejaculated. "Hey fuck my boyfriend, I'm good for now," Rob said to Jarold.

I wasn't really in the mood to get fucked by that big tool either after I shot my load.

"Oh, no thanks. Same here. Nothing personal Jarold but I can't take your cock right now after cumming."

"What's wrong with you guys, you don't like my cock ? I didn't cum yet," Jarold complained. I scooped my cum off my stomach with my right hand and used it as lube on Jarold's cock. I stroked him hard and fast but this guy had some stamina. After working his monster for ten minutes, my arm started hurting and I stopped.

"What's the matter ass hole, don't want to finish me off after I fucked your pussy ass faggot boyfriend ? Think you better than me or what ?"

I looked at Rob to see his reaction. He looked angry enough to punch Jarold's nuts.

"I show you who is the pussy ass faggot. You better get out of here now before I rip your fucking cock off," Rob yelled at him.

Jarold took his t-shirt of the floor and acted like he is getting dressed. Suddenly he swung his fist in Rob's face, but Rob moved his head to the side and missed most of the impact.

"Brian get my Taser, quick," Rob shouted to me. I jumped over to the dresser and opened the drawer, where Rob kept his Taser gun. I threw it over to Rob. He grabbed the Taser and yelled at Jarold :

"Come on make my day. I'm going to fry your fucking balls."

Jarold grabbed me by my right arm, put his left hand around my neck and tried to choke me. When Rob saw him doing this to me, he tasered his cock and his big balls. Jarold screamed and fell to the floor, holding his fuck tool with both hands. The electro shock must've forced his cum load out of his nuts because there was a massive cum puddle on the floor. It's ironic but Rob made him cum after all. Rob and I dragged him outside by his legs and left him on the curb.

"Damn what a nutcase. I don't even want to think what could have happened to you if you were alone with that idiot. I have enough from this bullshit. No more hookups babe. Only you and me," Rob said.

"I love you so much baby boy. That fucker scared the shit out of me," I whispered to Rob.

"His damn cock was too fat, now my ass hole is sore and hurting."

"Aw poor baby, you need first aid ? I'm good at it, let me see," I said to Rob.

"No, take your paws and dick off my hole. It needs a little rest, that's all. You better get your shit hole ready for my cock tomorrow," Rob lectured me.

It was almost six o'clock in the morning when our first night as boyfriends ended. We cuddled up in our bed and fell asleep.

Around noon Rob woke me up.

"Hey babe wake up. I'm horny and hungry. Want to have brunch in bed ? I make it if you want. And after brunch we do what boyfriends usually do. Fucking. I mean making love, sorry. You know what that is, right my baby ? You spread your butt cheeks and I put my erect penis on your ass hole. Slowly but steady I keep pushing the entire length of my rod into your rectum. I push it back and fore until my semen sprays out of my cum slit and that's how I inseminate you. You want to try ? I can teach you," Rob was joking around.

"If there is one thing you don't have to teach me, that is taking a man's cock up my fuck hole and milk him silly," I said to Rob.

He made brunch for us both. Hash browns, ham steak, toast and eggs.

After we ate I gave Rob a long sloppy kiss. It turned me on so much, I raised my butt hole up and pulled my ass cheeks apart. Robs cock didn't stay soft at this sight. He wanted to penetrate me laying on our sides so I changed position. He snuggled up from behind me, holding me in his arms, kissing my neck, sniffing and licking my armpits. I felt his hard cock poking and pushing against my tight, still closed fuck hole. The tip was wet from his precum and lubed up my hole very well. He started pushing harder, slowly pushing his head through my hole. He felt the resistance of my ass weakening as his head popped completely through my sphincter. I took a deep breath and enjoyed every millimeter and second of Rob's penis inside of me. I could feel his cock massaging my prostate, squeezing precum out of my dick. He made me produce my own lube to stroke my cock. Rob pumped his cock faster into my ass, started to sweat and breath harder, whispered how much he loved me and that he is inseminating me with all his seed and love. At that point I smelled his sweaty armpits and the sweet musky smell of his hairy crotch. His ecstatic man scent made me feel like melting wax being shaped by his hard pounding cock. It felt like Rob and I were one entity. Sex never felt as good before as with Rob.

He bucked his hips, his cock began to pulsate and I enjoyed the feeling of his seed filling up the inside of my love tunnel.

He was the first man who made me cum just by pounding my ass. I shot my load only a few seconds after he did. I was so overwhelmed by feelings of lust and love, I had tears in my eyes when I sprayed my cum on Rob's hand. When he saw my tears, he licked them off my cheeks followed by my cum on his hand.

"Rob, this was the best sex I ever had. Thank you for coming into my life."

"Same here baby boy, it was amazing," Rob whispered in my ear.

We took a few days off from work and enjoyed being together. Going shopping, having ice cream on the beach at sunset or going for a walk in the evening. And of course we had sex, a lot of sex.

Saturday night, it was already around nine, Jimmy called and asked if he can crash at mine and Robs house. He was arguing with Nick again. I told him yes but I need to ask Rob too. I told him I call back after talking to Rob.

"Hey babe, Jimmy asked if he can crash here tonight. They were arguing again."

"You know I'm not really crazy about your ex or whatever he is, but if it's only for one night I guess I can put up with him," Rob answered.

I called Jimmy and told him to come over. One hour later he was at the front door. We went into the living room where Rob was sitting on the couch. Jimmy has been jealous of Rob since I can remember, he always thought there was more between me and him than just friendship. I didn't tell him yet that Rob and I were together as boyfriends since one week. But it became more obvious the longer I knew him, that Jimmy was only coming to me when he needed a place to stay.

"Brian," Jimmy said, "want to go to your bedroom and I fuck you ?"

I didn't expect that and I looked over to Rob. He was getting angrier and more jealous by the minute. I like when someone gets jealous. To me it's proof that your partner loves you. In most cases at least.

Rob couldn't be quiet any longer.

"I don't think so Jim, Brian and I are together since last week. If somebody is fucking him, than it's me. You're just using him anyway."

Jimmy couldn't say a word. From his eyes I saw tears running down his cheeks.

"It's ok Jimmy," I tried to calm him down. "I wanted to tell you tonight. But you left me first, remember ?"

Jimmy understood, at least he tried.

"Are we good," I asked him. "We can be friends, I would like that a lot."

I saw some jealousy flickering in Rob's eyes.

"Yeah friends with benefits the way I know Jim. I don't think that's a good idea," Rob said.

"Don't worry babe, I won't cheat on you," I promised him. Rob and I went in our bedroom and Jimmy stayed in the spare bedroom.

Next morning Jimmy called Nick and everything was back to normal as I predicted. He went to work from our house.

Robs mom called later in the day and they talked something about visiting. After Rob hung up the phone he asked me :

"Baby girl, my mom asked if we want to come up to Missouri and visit her for a few days. Would you like to go ?"

"Baby girl ? I show you what that girl has between her legs. But yes sure, it would be nice to get away for a few days."

"Ok. We could leave this coming Friday and stay until Tuesday or so."

We arrived in St. Louis around ten pm Friday night. I noticed Robs mood changed a few times that day. When we were only one hour south of St. Louis, I saw him even cry. I thought he is probably excited to see his mom again and those are tears of happiness.

His mom opened the door when she saw us pulling in the driveway.

"Hi boys, how was the trip," she asked. She gave Rob and me a big hug.

"Come in, I still have some leftovers from dinner if you boys are hungry."

But we were just tired. We were sitting on her porch and talked for awhile before we went to bed.

The next day we planned to see the Gateway Arch. Rob and his mom had been inside at the top of the Arch a few years back, when Rob was still living in St. Louis but I had never been. From the top of the Gateway Arch I had a great view of the city. Later we had lunch at Robs mom favorite diner.

Rob and I shared a big portion of beef stew. I fed Rob with my spoon and he fed me with his.

"Come on, open your big mouth Brian," Rob mumbled.

"The spoon is too big Rob, go slow."

"Are you kidding me, you never complained about something too big in your mouth before," Rob said and grinned.

His mom seemed a little embarrassed about it but nobody really cared. At the table across from us, two guys had lunch together and smiled at us, when they saw us feeding each other.

Rob was unusual quiet that morning and had a sad look on his face.

"What's the matter Rob," I asked him.

"Nothing, really. I just feel tired. When we get home we could take a nap together," Rob was whispering and blinked with his left eye.

"Oh your mind is in the gutter again. Not in your mom's house and your sisters room," was my answer.

Robs hands were shaking when we left the diner and he looked pale.

"Brian can you drive, I feel suddenly light headed and get cold sweat."

"Sure, no problem babe."

When we got back home, Rob was laying down on the couch but couldn't sleep. After two hours, he complained about pain in his lower abdomen. I told him to go to bed, I would be there in a few. He got off the couch and walked slowly upstairs. I went back to the kitchen to get him an chamomile tea, when I heard something fall. I figured Rob dropped his shoes. Five minutes later I grabbed the cup of tea and walked upstairs.

The bathroom door was open and Rob was laying unconscious on the bathroom floor.

"Rob, can you hear me," I screamed. But he didn't move. "Maggy, call 911. Rob is not responding," I yelled. Robs mom called 911. Five minutes later the ambulance arrived. They took Rob to the nearest hospital. I followed them in my car. Robs mom said she's coming to the hospital after she was done dying her hair.

When I got to the ER, Rob was already in a single room. He was conscious again but couldn't talk clearly.

"Babe, what happened. You scared the shit out of me. You ok ?" Rob tried to say something to me but he was to weak. He said "That is Space ball, can you hear it ?" I didn't hear anything. He must have dreamed. The doctor just got the results from Rob's blood test. There was an infection in Rob's body. They had to find out where it was very soon. After a few more tests and x-rays, the doctor talked to me.

"Your friends appendix ruptured. One hour later and he wouldn't be alive. You saved his life," the doctor told me. After the surgery, Rob and I were alone in the room. I looked at Rob lying on the bed, wearing only a hospital gown. I looked at him and got a boner. I was sliding both of my hands under the cover and played with Rob's cock and ass. I didn't know there were cameras installed in his room. After 5 min. a nurse entered the room and said in a harsh tone: "It maybe looks different on the monitor, than what you're actually doing. But you should keep your hands above the blanket. I turned red as a lobster. Every nurse on the station could see me fondling Rob on their monitors. After 25 min a male nurse came in and said it may be better when I come back another time. Rob started to get angry. He said

"If we were a straight couple, nobody would care or say anything."

"It's ok Rob," I tried to calm him down. "I go home and pick you up in the morning when they release you."

He started crying again. "I don't want you to leave babe." I didn't know what to say. "I have to go baby boy, you heard what the nurse said. I would rather stay here with you of course." I gave him a kiss and didn't care about the camera. Rob seemed depressed and sad, I hadn't seen him like this before.

"See ya tomorrow babe." I left and went back to his mom's house.

I told her that Rob would be released the next morning. It was the first night I had to sleep alone since we were together. I was horny as hell. I found one of Rob's worn boxers on the floor. I picked them up and laid down on the bed. I was holding them in my hand and thought about Rob's dick and ball sack had been hanging and rubbing against the fabric. Where the tip of his cock usually touches the boxers, there was a cum stain. Rob must've been precumming while we were driving yesterday. My dick was precumming and hard right now just from thinking about Rob's cock. I pulled my pants down and sniffed on his boxers where the cum stain was. Robs crotch produced this intoxicating sweet musky smell. I pulled my foreskin back and was rubbing my knob, thinking about Rob and the sexual experiments we still wanted to try. I put his boxers on my nose, in my left hand I was holding my phone and took a video of myself stroking off. When I got closer to ejaculate, I used my foreskin to finish myself off. I pulled the skin up and down with a tight grip of my fist. I was about to cum when I took a close up of my cock, shooting the creamy hot semen on my stomach. I moaned and talked to myself : "Here baby, that's all for you." The video was only one minute and twenty two seconds long. I sent it to Robs phone so he could have some fun too. About twenty minutes later, Rob texted back :"Thanks you horny little fucker. See you soon. Love you baby boy."

It was around 2.30 am when the hospital called and told me, Rob disappeared. I got dressed immediately and jumped in the truck. I drove up and down the streets near the hospital and found him sitting on the curb in front of a McDonald's.

"What are you doing here babe, you should be in the hospital." Rob just looked at me but didn't say anything. "Rob what's the matter ?" He got off the ground and started crying. "I had to get out of there."

"Why ?" I asked him.

"I don't know, I had the feeling."

"Ok. I didn't think my video would result in that reaction. Come in, we go home," and I smiled at him. He got in the truck but didn't smile, instead he said :"Do you work together with them ? You bringing me back to the hospital, do you ?"

"What are you talking about ?"

I didn't know what else to say. When we parked in his mom's driveway, he came down and said: "I'm so happy to be back home with you."

We went upstairs and jumped in our bed.

I woke up early the next morning. Rob wasn't on his side of the bed. I went to the bathroom to take a piss. Rob was laying naked on the floor and jerking his cock. He looked at me and said: "Morning babe, wanna join me ?" I was kinda pissed at him and asked: "Why are you jerking off in here ? We or you could've done it together. You rather stroke yourself then making love with me ?"

"No baby boy, I was so horny from watching your jerk off video, I wanted to try it myself and return the favor." I didn't expect that answer and tried to cover up the fact that I was mad. "Aw, you're so sweet babe. Thank you. Well I guess I let you finish and send the vid to me."

I went downstairs to the kitchen and made coffee. Rob came ten minutes later. "Damn that took long. How many times did you cum," I asked him but he only said "just once." We sat down at the table and had our coffee and a cigarette.

"Brian," he said, "I would rather drive back home today. I'm feeling tired and weak. Maybe it wasn't a good idea to come up here." I was surprised because he was excited to see his mom again. I really didn't care if we go home sooner. "Sure baby, if you wanna go today, I have no problem with that."

We left that afternoon and drove back to Florida.

"HEY ROB, YOU KNOW WHAT, maybe we should have one big last group sex orgie with ten or fifteen naked guys fucking each other silly."

"Really Brian, didn't we agree never again a third or more after the last time with that crazy fucker ?"

"Yeah I know, was just an idea. We can think about it later," was all I answered. Finally at 9 AM the next day, we were home. Rob had to lay down on the couch and fell asleep. I unpacked the few things we had on our trip. Rob was snoring and I saw his cock getting hard in his pants. It was always my fantasy to jerk off a sleeping guy. I was curious if a man can shoot a load while sleeping. The problem is, most guys wake up. But Rob was a sound sleeper, so my chances were good.

I kneeled next to the couch and very carefully opened his zipper. The button was next. So far he was still snoring. His cock pitched a big tent in his boxers. I pulled the waistband down and his dick jumped out, standing hard and veiny in front of my face. I touched it careful and it jumped up a few times. I put his head between my thumb and index finger and rubbed it soft at first. I got bolder when he was still sleeping and moved my fingers faster and with a tighter grip up and down. That was the moment when he started to move and put his left hand on his balls. His cock was pulsating and from the tip was a steady flow of stringy precum dripping down on his hairy belly. He moved again and I heard him moan. It was time for me to get my meat out of my pants and rub one out.

I was distracted pulling my own cock out, when Rob's cock turned dark red and started to blow his hot seed. I didn't even do five strokes, when I felt my cum rising up my shaft. I got off my knees and pushed my cock on Rob's lips. His mouth was half open and I pumped my jizz on his tongue and lips. I couldn't help it, but I made a loud high pitch sound that woke up Rob.

"Damn babe, why are you waking me up ? What the hell is that stuff in my mouth, it tastes like cum." He wiped my cum with his left hand from his lips and he must have swallowed, what had been in his mouth. Then he finally noticed my dick hanging out of my pants.

"No you didn't, you horny little fucker. And it looks and feels like you milked me too. As your punishment for being so sneaky, you have to lick my cum from my belly."

"Punishment ? Oh yeah, ok. That's really a bad, bad punishment Rob. How can you make me do something nasty like that ?" I licked from Rob's pubic hairline up to his belly button and sucked up all of his sperm.

"Thanks' for punishing me babe," I joked around.

"Welcome dumbass," Rob mumbled, and thank you for waking me up that way. Was hot."

But Rob didn't really act and look like he did enjoy it. He had this sad look on his face again.

"What's the matter baby boy ?" I asked Rob.

"Sorry babe but I just don't feel good. My nuts are hurting since a few days."

"Why didn't you say something to me Rob ?"

"I didn't want to worry you. I thought it's gone in a day or so."

"Well if it's a few days already you should go to a doctor. Let me see your balls." I checked his nuts with my fingers and I could feel a lump on his left testicle. It also seemed bigger than it was before.

"Damn Rob, you're growing bull balls down here," I joked, not to worry him. " No, I'm ok. Give me a few more days and I will jump your bones again like an eight weeks old pup."

It was senseless to argue with him. Two weeks later, Rob's balls were still hurting. Not to mention, we had no sex at all. I stroked my cock every day in front of him, but he wasn't in any mood to lend me his hand or take care of his dick.

He finally agreed to make an appointment for him after three more weeks. The soonest available appointment was five days later. We drove together to the clinic. Rob was nervous and scared. So was I but I tried not to show it. At two pm the doctor called Rob into his office.

"Brian can you come with me ?" he asked me. I followed him and sat down on a chair next to the exam bed.

"First I need to draw some blood and then I take a x-ray of your testicles Mr. Rob," the doctor explained to him. Rob was a chicken when it came to doctors, hospitals or blood. I saw the pure horror in his beautiful brown eyes, when he heard about drawing blood.

"Babe can you hold my hand please," he asked me. I was holding his right hand when the nurse drew some blood from his left arm. Rob was pale as shit. After that cruel procedure, the doc told Rob to pull his pants down and lay back on the bed. He put something that looked like a wooden butcher block between Rob's legs and put his sack on top of it. He took the x-ray and Rob was done. He told Rob to call the next day, when they had the results from the lab.

Rob had me call there on the next day of course. The doctor said Rob needs to come back to the clinic again. We both drove over to the clinic. The doctor was waiting in his office. "Hi Rob, I wanted you to come back because I have good news and bad news. Are you two a couple ? The bad news are, it's testicular cancer and the good news are, we can remove the testicle and if the cancer didn't spread into the surrounding area, there is a 99% chance of being cancer free."

Rob was too shocked to say anything. I asked the doctor about the procedure and set a date for the surgery. I was holding Rob's hand on the way home. He still didn't say a word. I pulled into the garage. He jumped out of the truck and went in our bedroom. I thought I give him a few minutes by himself. About ten minutes later he came into the living room and finally talked.

"I'm not having my nuts cut off babe. How much of a man would I be without my balls. I will get fat and have no sex drive. How could I satisfy you. You need to look for another man in your life. Another partner. I can't be with you or anybody else ever again."

I was shocked about what he just said.

"Babe, I don't want anybody else. I want you for the rest of our lives. And I don't care if you have one, two or no balls at all. If you don't have them removed, you will die. I think the second choice to live without them is still better, don't you think ?"

"I'm not sure about that," Rob answered.

The surgery was in four days. Rob changed his mind and agreed to the surgery. Unfortunately they had to cut off both of his nuts.

Friday morning, the day of surgery, Rob was crying and depressed. I was holding him in my arms and we both cried.

"We got to go babe," I said to Rob. "Let's get it over with, you will be back home tomorrow."

"Sounds good. Are you really sure you want to live with me even when I'm castrated ?"

Rob's phone was ringing. "It's the hospital. They can't get me there soon enough I guess."

"Don't you want to pick up," I asked.

"Nah, it's ok. Let's go." My phone was ringing right after Rob's stopped. It was the hospital again. I picked up and Robs doctor told me, they made a mistake and the cancer patient is not Rob. I thanked him hundred times and hung up the phone.

"Ok babe, want to get castrated ?" I joked.

"Oh shut up dumbass," Rob said and started crying.

"I was kidding Rob. The hospital called to let you know, it was a mistake and you don't have cancer."

Rob was screaming for joy and gave me a big hug and kiss. "You know, that idea you had about having a group sex party for the last time, we should do it as a celebration in honor of keeping my nuts," Rob said.

"Yeah one last time. We don't have to have sex with other guys, we can watch them and only you and I play together. That way I don't get jealous about someone who puts his cock in your ass," was my response.

We planned the party for the next weekend. We weren't sure about the theme yet. My favorite was 'Let the sling begin to swing' or Rob's favorite 'Nuts and Bolts.'

We agreed on 'Nuts and Bolts' from 11pm - 1am and 'Let the sling begin to swing' from 1am - 3am.

I wanted everything perfect and the party to be an unforgettable event. We invited eight horny gay guys and our three friends Sir Ryan, his alpha sub Mark and their boy pup. They just bought an old industrial park and converted it into a Training Camp for men who want to become a sex slave or a filthy sex pig. They used to host great sex dinner parties. Rob and I were planning to visit their new Camp since they had opened, but never got the chance. Rob and I plus eleven guests makes thirteen together.

Thirteen is the lucky number used in connection with dark, twisted group sex orgies.

Sir Ryan, Mark and their boy pup arrived four hours earlier than anybody else. I wanted them to help Rob and me to set up the play area. I called them 'the masters of group sex party organization.' Right next to the entrance door we put a small table with condoms, lube and poppers on it. The 'Toy box' was in the corner behind the door. The sling we hung in front of the glass slider doors so our gay neighbors could do their favorite thing and watch us fucking. We also put a big black rubber mattress on the living room floor.

It was almost eleven pm and the other guests should arrive soon.

"Well, let's get naked guys or do you want to greet our guests fully dressed. That would be perversion pure," Rob announced. The other eight men arrived shortly one after another and got also undressed without losing any time.

"Hey babe," I said to Rob, "we should try our sounding experiment tonight, you want to ?"

"Fuck yeah baby boy." I walked over to the toy box and choose a hollow steel rod. Rob and I were standing in the center of the room, facing each other. Rob's cock was already hard. I grabbed his nuts, holding and slightly squeezing them. "I'm so glad I still can play with your balls and they didn't get cut off," I whispered to Rob.

I inserted the one end of the steel sound into Rob's piss slit and pushed it down his urethra until half of the rod disappeared inside his shaft. The other end I pushed down my own cock and when I had about half of the sound inside my dick, Rob's and my head were touching each other. Our cocks were impaled by a steel hollow rod. It was hot to look at. "Hey Sir Ryan, you need to take a pic of Rob's and Brian's cock getting fucked by each other from the inside," the boy pup suggested. "You stand right next to them, bend over, spread your ass cheeks and show them both your fuck hole," Sir Ryan ordered his boy. He was a cute little pup with some silky black fur between his ass cheeks. He came over to Rob and me and pulled his cheeks apart so Rob and I could see his pink hole. I pulled my foreskin over Robs head and began to stroke our cocks. Rob pushed his left middle finger in the pups fuck hole and massaged his prostate until his precum was dripping on the floor. "Look Brian, the pup didn't get castrated either," Rob said and laughed. Sir Ryan took a pic of us three in that position. I looked in Rob's face and I knew he was enjoying the sounding and stroking while having his finger buried inside a tight fuck tube. "Babe I'm going to cum, I'm going to cum now," Rob yelled and his seed traveled from his cock through the hollow steel rod into my cock.

This took me over the edge and I released my sperm load. My cum pushed Rob's semen out of my dick, back through the sound into his cock. Rob had two loads of cum in his cock. We pulled the rod out of our dicks. "Where did the cum go Brian," Rob asked me. "I don't know, it's probably stuck in your tubing somewhere," I answered him.

In the meantime two of the guys got busy in the sling. Sir Ryan and Mark were planning to give a demonstration on how to humiliate, edge and milk a man. From a hook in the ceiling they had a rope hanging down. A hairy stud with a hot looking cock and low hanging bull balls was hanging from the rope, his arms tied behind his back. Mark put a red rag into the guy's mouth so the neighbors wouldn't hear him scream when he got milked. Sir Ryan hit the guy's dick head, using a thin bamboo stick. I heard the muffled sound of a scream, coming from the stud. Mark worked on his ass hole, fucking him with a baseball bat. Sir Ryan kept working on his cock. With his right thumb and index finger he rubbed up and down the guys cock head. "The sooner you give me your cum, the sooner I can use it as lube on your cock," Sir Ryan said. "But remember it will hurt your sensitive dick head after you cum and believe me, I won't stop milking until I get at least three loads out of you. Don't even ask me to stop." Sir Ryan didn't have to wait long for the first cum load. He held his hand underneath the guys dick head and collected the semen on the palm of his hand. After the milkee was done squirting, Ryan grabbed his cock with his fist and stroked his dick, lubing it up well with the hot fresh sperm. The poor guy screamed and tried to pull his cock away from Ryan's fist. But his fist was holding on tight and kept stroking the sensitive head, milking the next load out of those big hairy bull balls. The guy was sweating and screaming to stop, but Sir Ryan just smacked his nuts every time he wanted him to stop. Mark was still fucking the milkee with the baseball bat. His ass juices were oozing out and made a excellent lube. With one forceful push, Mark slammed the wooden baseball bat deep into his ass. That caused the guy to ejaculate his second load, but that time it sprayed on the living room floor. A lean young tattooed stud scooped up the cum from the floor, using only his finger. He also used it as lube on his cock. He must've been so excited about another man's cum on his cock, he emptied his nuts immediately. He shot his cum on the guys dick, who was fucking someone in the sling, adding his own homemade lube. In the meantime Rob put Sir Ryan's boy pup on a chain and hooked it to a chair. He plugged the rubber puppy tail into his ass. I could hear the boy breathing sharp, when Rob pushed the big plug part inside the hole. It filled the pups tight ass well. Someone manhandled the boy pups dick and ball sack from behind with his black leather boots.

"Hey all you horny guys, how about we put Ryan's boy pup in the sling and y'all run a train on him," Rob shouted. The pup was dragged to the sling. The two guys who used it before just got done. "Jump in," Mark said to his boy. He climbed on the sling with the pup tail still wagging in his ass. The first man running the train pulled the tail out. "Damn that plug stretched his fucking pup hole to the max," the man said. "I have to wait a few if I want it nice and tight. But what the hell, ass is ass," and he pushed his cock inside the boys pink and stretched hairy ass. When everyone of us was done seeding the pup hole, Mark said : "Now push it all out, all twelve fucking slimy loads, push it, come on. Give us back our seed."

The boy's hole opened up and the semen of twelve men was gushing out. I was holding a glass bowl underneath his freshly fucked ass and most of the twelve loads splashed down in it. I held the bowl up above my head and announced : "Guys, we going to have a circle jerk. The first guy shooting his load can drink all the cum in the bowl after each of us nutted his seed into it. That makes twenty-four loads. So who is the lucky bastard. Go ahead guys, time is starting now."

Everybody was whacking their dicks like there was a gold trophy to win. I didn't believe it, but Rob was the first one who unloaded his white, hot gold. He added it into the bowl and one after another gave up his seed. Rob was about to drink twenty-four loads. "Rob, if you drink all this, you going to piss cum in the next two days," I said into the crowd. Rob put the bowl to his mouth and emptied it in one big gulp. Everybody applauded when the bowl was empty.

"Thank you guys, y'all left a pleasant taste in my mouth," Rob said and laughed. "My baby boy Brian and I thank you so much for joining our sex party. From now on we will make love only to each other. That doesn't mean we won't join any parties no more, but we will only watch others play.

You guys are welcome to watch Brian and me fuck each other of course. Thank you Sir Ryan and Mark for your invitation to visit you and your Training Camp soon."

At 3.30 AM everybody was gone. Rob and I went to bed and snuggled up to each other. We were curious about the Training Camp Ryan and Mark bought. He told us it used to be 'Bergen Industrial Park' somewhere in the midwest bible belt.

When we woke up next morning I talked to Rob about buying property outside the city limits. He liked the idea and the next day we put our house on the market. We didn't know where to stay when it sells, but a hotel or campground would be good enough until we found the right property.

The realtor found a buyer after only two weeks. The closing date was set four days later.

When we got to the title insurance office, our realtor and buyer were already there.

Our realtor told us, he just got a mobile home on a quarter acre of land for sale. It wasn't even listed yet. And the price was outstanding. We looked at the property right after the closing. It had a lot of Cypress trees, two ponds, and a wooden privacy fence all around.

"That's our smaller version of a Training Camp," Rob laughed.

"This property is the start of our new life babe, Rob whispered in my ear.

This book covered the years 2010 – 2016.
Part two will continue from 2016 until the present.

# Don't miss out!

Visit the website below and you can sign up to receive emails whenever T. Brian Loos publishes a new book. There's no charge and no obligation.

https://books2read.com/r/B-A-DUVY-LFTNC

**BOOKS 2 READ**

Connecting independent readers to independent writers.

# Also by T. Brian Loos

Say My Name Boy
Sir Ryan and Mark
The Miracle Drug - Crystal Meth / English & German Edition
Island of Men
My Straight Buddy
Post-WWII in Germany
The Prison Dungeon
Breeding Camp Of No Return
The Witch Broom Flight & Landing Manual for Advanced
German & English Edition
Dickipedia
Puppers Lane
Bound by Twisted Passion

# About the Author

T. Brian Loos was born and raised in Frankfurt Germany. In 1998 he moved to Tampa, Fl.

where he started his own business. His first book was "The Miracle Drug" Crystal Meth, followed by the gay erotic story "The Christmas Dinner Party."

Readers liked his first story so much, they suggested to write another chapter, which was the "New Years Dinner Party" and the series "Sir Ryan and Mark" was born. He found his genre in writing Erotic Short Stories for the LGBT community.